HARRIET ZIEFERT

Illustrated by Donald Saaf

Elemenopeo

HOUGHTON MIFFLIN COMPANY BOSTON

1998

For animals who shared our house —
Puffy, Helen, Pushkin.
— D.S.

Walter Lorraine (wл) Books

Text copyright © 1998 by Harriet Ziefert
Illustrations copyright © 1998 by Donald Saaf

Library of Congress Cataloguing-in-Publication Data

Ziefert, Harriet.
    Elomenopeo / written by Harriet Ziefert and illustrated
by Donald Saaf.
        p.   cm.
    Summary: In the house alone, an unusual cat named
Elomenopeo paints a picture and then curls up to dream.
    ISBN 0-395-90493-5
    [1. Cats – Fiction. 2. Painting – Fiction.] I. Saaf, Donald,
1937– ill. II. Title.
PZ7. Z487E1   1998
[E]   dc21   97-47277
                                                        CIP
                                                        AC

Printed in China for Harriet Ziefert, Inc.
HZI 10 9 8 7 6 5 4 3 2 1

My name is Elemenopeo.
If you don't know how to say my name, just read
these letters: L...M...N...O...P...O.

I may look like an ordinary cat. But I'm not. I always get up early and eat breakfast. Today I'm having a bagel with lox and cream cheese.

After I eat, I let myself out of the house through my
own special door. I like being free to come and go
as I please.

I take a quick walk around the yard to be sure no bad guys have wandered in. Then I'm ready for bird-watching. I'm smart. I know names of lots of different ones, like finch, grackle, and blue jay.

I try to get the birds to play hide-and-seek.
"Hey, don't fly away!" I cry. "I'm just playing. It's a game."
But the birds don't believe me.

Instead of eating lunch, I take a nap.

I dream of flying.

In the afternoon a cat friend usually comes by and we play cat games.

Sometimes, if I'm unlucky, a mean dog tries to get me. But I know how to escape.

Through the cat door and back into the house!

I'm an orderly cat. I like the sameness of my days—outside
every morning for hours in the garden with the birds.
But today is different. My special door is shut...closed for repairs.
I can't open it. I can't go out.

I don't know what to do. I feel cooped up. I prowl
from room to room, looking for something interesting.

Then I see an easel. And a box of paints.

I put on a smock.

I dip my paw into blue.

I get my brush and palette.

And I begin.

I could paint a tree, or a house, or a flower,
or a bagel, or a mean dog. But I won't.

I'd rather paint a picture of myself...

me, Elemenopeo...
with wings!

Then I step back to take a look at my picture.
Wow! It's good. I like it. I'm an artist!

I sign my name big. If anyone wants to know,

I'll tell them the title: *Portrait of the Artist as a Young Bird.*

Painting a large picture can make a small cat tired.

I need to rest. So I'm going to curl up and...

dream.